Dear Parents and Educators,

Welcome to Penguin Young Readers! As parents and educators, you know that each child develops at his or her own pace—in terms of speech, critical thinking, and, of course, reading. Penguin Young Readers recognizes this fact. As a result, each Penguin Young Readers book is assigned a traditional easy-to-read level (1–4) as well as a Guided Reading Level (A–P). Both of these systems will help you choose the right book for your child. Please refer to the back of each book for specific leveling information. Penguin Young Readers features esteemed authors and illustrators, stories about favorite characters, fascinating nonfiction, and more!

Cork & Fuzz: Spring Cleaning

LEVEL **3**

GUIDED READING LEVEL **J**

This book is perfect for a **Transitional Reader** who:
- can read multisyllable and compound words;
- can read words with prefixes and suffixes;
- is able to identify story elements (beginning, middle, end, plot, setting, characters, problem, solution); and
- can understand different points of view.

Here are some **activities** you can do during and after reading this book:
- Compare/Contrast: In this book, Cork and Fuzz have two totally different views on spring cleaning. For instance, spring cleaning makes Cork very excited, but it makes Fuzz very tired. Compare and contrast the two friends' views on spring cleaning to show how they are different and how they are alike.
- Creative Writing: At the end of this book, Cork and Fuzz made up rules for their club, such as "no bossing" and "no spitting." Pretend you are part of their club, too. Write a list of ten rules that you would make for your club. Make sure they are only good rules!

Remember, sharing the love of reading with a child is the best gift you can give!

—Bonnie Bader, EdM
   Penguin Young Readers program

*Penguin Young Readers are leveled by independent reviewers applying the standards developed by Irene Fountas and Gay Su Pinnell in *Matching Books to Readers: Using Leveled Books in Guided Reading*, Heinemann, 1999.

For Aeryn and Cameron—DC

To Shem, my little book lover!—LM

PENGUIN YOUNG READERS
An Imprint of Penguin Random House LLC

Penguin supports copyright. Copyright fuels creativity, encourages diverse voices,
promotes free speech, and creates a vibrant culture. Thank you for buying an authorized edition
of this book and for complying with copyright laws by not reproducing, scanning, or distributing
any part of it in any form without permission. You are supporting writers and allowing Penguin
to continue to publish books for every reader.

Text copyright © 2015 by Dori Chaconas. Illustrations copyright © 2015 by Lisa McCue.
All rights reserved. Previously published in hardcover in 2015 by Penguin Young Readers.
This paperback edition published in 2016 by Penguin Young Readers, an imprint of
Penguin Random House LLC, 345 Hudson Street, New York, New York 10014.
Manufactured in China.

Library of Congress Control Number: 2014015816

ISBN 978-0-448-48126-5   10 9 8 7 6 5 4 3 2 1

CORK & FUZZ

Spring Cleaning

by Dori Chaconas
illustrated by Lisa McCue

Penguin Young Readers
An Imprint of Penguin Random House

Chapter 1

Cork was a short muskrat.

He liked to clean.

Spring cleaning made him
very, very happy.

Fuzz was a tall possum.

He did not like to clean.

Spring cleaning made him
very, very tired.

Two best friends.

One always ready to work hard.

The other one hardly ever ready
to work.

On the first warm day of spring,

Cork ran to Fuzz's house.

"Fuzz!" Cork called up into the tree.

"Wake up!

It is time for spring cleaning!"

Fuzz stuck his head out of his house.

He yawned.

"Why?" he asked.

"Because when winter is over it is

time to clean," Cork said.

"Why?" Fuzz asked again.

"To clean up fallen branches and twigs," Cork said.

"To make our yards and houses ready for spring."

All at once, sticks, twigs, and leaves
flew out of Fuzz's house.

They fell all over the ground.

They fell all over Cork.

"What are you doing?" Cork yelled.

"Cleaning," Fuzz said.

He threw out one last leaf.

"All done!"

"You made a mess," Cork said.

"That is not a mess," Fuzz answered.

"That is my bed.

I am airing it out."

"We can clean my yard next,"
Cork said.

"Nuts!" Fuzz said.

Chapter 2

Cork pulled Fuzz to Cork's yard.

Cork hopped and skipped.

Fuzz yawned and moaned.

"We can pick up all these branches
and twigs," Cork said.
"We can make a brush pile next
to that rock."
Cork pointed to a big, heavy branch.
"I will lift this end," he said to Fuzz.
"You take that end.
We will work together."

Cork lifted his end of the branch.

He pulled.

"Oof!"

The branch did not move.

Cork pulled harder.

The branch still did not move.

Cork looked back at Fuzz.

Fuzz was sitting on the end
of the branch.

"What are you doing, Fuzz?"
Cork yelled.

"I am tired," Fuzz said.

"I am waiting for a ride.

You are not pulling very fast."

Cork stamped his foot.

"We are not riding," he said.

"We are cleaning!"

"Okay, okay!" said Fuzz.

They pulled the branch

to the big rock.

Cork picked up more branches.

He threw them on the brush pile.

Fuzz picked up a leaf.

He threw it on the brush pile.

The wind picked up Fuzz's leaf.

It blew it back into the yard.

"Nuts!" Fuzz said.

Fuzz chased the leaf.

He jumped on it.

There was something under the leaf.

"Look, Cork!" Fuzz said.

"Look what I found!"

Chapter 3

"I found three stones for my

collection," Fuzz said.

"We are not looking for stones!"

Cork said.

"We are cleaning!"

Cork threw more twigs on the

brush pile.

Fuzz went down to the pond.

He splashed in the water.

"You are not cleaning," Cork called.

"Yes, I am!" Fuzz said.

"I am cleaning my new stones."

Cork groaned.

"I thought you were too tired

to clean," he said.

"I am too tired for your kind of
cleaning," Fuzz said.

"And now I am hungry, too!
I am hungry and tired."

Then he stuck out his chin.

"And you are not the boss of me,"
Fuzz said.

Cork sighed.

"I know where there is a potato chip bag," Cork said.

"Would that help?

It still has potato chips in it.

But they might be stale."

"I like stale," Fuzz said.

"They might be soggy," Cork said.

"I like soggy," Fuzz said.

"Okay," Cork said.

"I will get the potato chip bag."

Cork followed the path through
the woods.

He followed it for a long, long time.

At last he came to a picnic area.

He pulled a potato chip bag
out of a trash bin.

When Cork got back to the pond,

his eyes opened wide.

The yard was clean!

It was very, very clean.

And the brush pile was very, very big!

But Fuzz was not there.

Fuzz was nowhere to be seen.

Chapter 4

"Fuzz is mad at me," Cork said.
"He is mad at me because I was
bossy.

Now my best friend is gone."

Cork sniffled and wiped his eyes.

"Maybe he is gone forever."

Snorzzz . . .

A noise came from

the big brush pile.

Snorzzz . . .

Cork walked around the brush pile.

He saw a small opening.

He crawled in.

And there was Fuzz,

sleeping and snoring.

Snorzzz . . .

"Oh, Fuzz!" Cork said.

"You did not go away!

You cleaned the whole yard!"

Fuzz opened his eyes.

He yawned.

"I did not clean," Fuzz said.

"I needed the branches and twigs
to build a nap house.

I am napping.

Go away."

Cork sat down next to Fuzz.

"I am sorry," Cork said.

"I am sorry for being bossy."

He held out the potato chip bag.

"It's okay," Fuzz said.

He took the bag.

Then he said,

"You like to clean.

I do not like to clean.

Sometimes we can

like different

things."

"And still be best friends," Cork said.

Fuzz nodded.

"And still be best friends," he said.

"I like your nap house," Cork said.

"It is like a clubhouse."

"What would we do in a clubhouse?"
Fuzz asked.

"We would make up club rules,"
Cork said.

"I do not like rules," Fuzz said.

"We would make up only good rules," Cork said.

"Rule number one: no bossing."

"Rule number two," said Fuzz.

"No spitting."

"You spit?" asked Cork.

"Not in the clubhouse," Fuzz answered.

"Are you still tired?" Cork asked.

"Nope," said Fuzz.

"We need to make up lots
and lots of good rules!"

And so they did.
Two best friends, making up
club rules and eating stale,
soggy potato chips.